W9-DGH-803

BILLY FORGET-ME-NOT

Billy
FORGET-ME-NOT

By

MAUDE M. TANNER, D.M.D.

Illustrated by

DOROTHEA J. SNOW

FOLLETT PUBLISHING COMPANY

Chicago, Illinois

Contents

Illustrations

Who Is Billy Forget-Me-Not?

CHAPTER
ONE

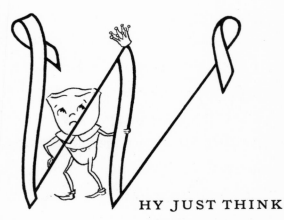

HY JUST THINK
Buddy, when you wake up tomorrow morning,
you'll be six years old! Your birthday party is
going to be lots of fun." Mother smiled, as she
tucked in the covers.

But Buddy didn't smile. Instead, he rubbed
his cheek and said, "It hurts here, Mother."

"Your gum does look a little swollen," Mother
said, as she looked in his mouth. "Try to go to

sleep, and maybe it will be all right in the morning. We've lots to do tomorrow."

Buddy shut his eyes tight; but try as he would, he could not fall off to sleep. There was so much to think about. All of his friends were coming to his birthday party. There would be cake and ice cream—and games—and PRESENTS!

But, oh, how his gum hurt! What if he couldn't eat the ice cream and cake at his party?

"I wish I could go to sleep," thought Buddy. And then he remembered. Daddy said he always counted sheep when he couldn't fall asleep. "Maybe I can count the bedposts," Buddy whispered to himself. "1...2...3..." he began to count.

And then he saw the strangest sight. There, perched on the fourth bedpost, was a little dwarf no bigger than Buddy's thumb. He was short and fat, and had the funniest little legs. About his neck he wore a pink collar and on his head a pearl crown.

"Heigh-ho!" he said, with a merry grin.

Buddy could not believe his ears. "Who . . . who are you?" he whispered, trying hard not to seem afraid.

The little dwarf shook his head until his pearl crown almost hid one merry blue eye.

"Oho!" he said, with a big smile, "that's for you to find out. You see, I have come to live with you. Why, I'll even be at your birthday party!" The dwarf was so friendly that Buddy began to feel more brave.

"Oh, will you?" he cried.

"To be sure," said the little dwarf, setting his pearl crown straight. "And what is more, I'll be one of your very best friends if you treat me right and keep my face clean."

"Keep your face clean?" asked Buddy. "How?"

"Why, scrub it every morning and night," was the answer. "You see, I'm too little to wash myself. And I have three brothers who also will come and live with you and be your friends. But you must promise to take very good care of us."

"Oh, I will, Mr. . . . uh . . . uh . . . Dwarf," said Buddy, who did not know yet what to call his little visitor.

"Call me Billy Forget-Me-Not. That means you must not forget to keep my face clean."

"All right, Billy. I'll keep your face clean. But I wish you would tell me who you are."

The little dwarf just laughed and smoothed his pink collar. "Some day you will know who I am. Now listen to my song—

Forget me not, and you shall see
How bright and clean my face will be."

Suddenly, Billy stopped singing. He hopped to his toes, waved his crown, and before Buddy's very eyes turned a somersault into the air and disappeared.

Buddy scrambled to the foot of the bed as fast as he could.

CRASH! BANG!

"Ouch!" cried Buddy, as he opened his eyes

"Ouch!" cried Buddy,
as he rubbed his head

12 and rubbed a sore spot on his head. For a moment he didn't know what had happened. Then he remembered the little dwarf. "Billy, Billy, where are you?"

Out of bed he jumped and began looking everywhere. He looked under the bed and beneath the pillows and bedcovers. He even looked in his shoes, and in his box of toys, and in his milk truck and his electric train.

"Billy Forget-Me-Not!" called Buddy. "Where are you? Why don't you answer me?"

Where COULD he be? And WHO was Billy Forget-Me-Not? He didn't look like a fairy, or a brownie either.

"He must be a really truly dwarf," said Buddy.

Just then Mother came in. "Happy birthday, Buddy," she said. "Why, what are you doing on the floor? Have you lost something?"

"I can't find Billy Forget-Me-Not," said Buddy.

"Billy who?" asked Mother.

"Billy Forget-Me-Not, a little dwarf who came

Buddy couldn't find the little dwarf anywhere

in the night and sat on the bedpost. Right here he sat and talked with me for the longest time," said Buddy. "He had funny little legs and a pearl crown and a pink collar."

Mother laughed. "I'm afraid it was only a dream, Buddy." But just the same she helped Buddy look for Billy Forget-Me-Not.

"Oh, Mother. Here he is! Here he is!" Buddy cried from the hall.

But before she could get there she heard Buddy say, "Oh, it isn't Billy at all. It's only Daddy's pearl tie-clip. He must have dropped it when he put on his coat."

They looked in every room in the house, but it was no use. They couldn't find the little dwarf anywhere.

"Come, Buddy," said Mother at last, "you must eat your breakfast. Your oatmeal is getting cold. We must get ready for your party."

"Oh, Billy's coming to my party!" cried Buddy. "He told me so."

Buddy's Birthday Party

CHAPTER
TWO

UDDY WAS SO EXCITED that he could hardly eat his breakfast. He had so many things to do before the party!

He picked out games and toys for his friends to play with. He hid the peanuts for the Treasure Hunt. He put some of the peanuts where they would be easy to find. But he grinned to himself as he put one in each of Daddy's rubbers. Who would ever think of looking there!

Suddenly, Buddy sniffed. What was that good smell coming from the kitchen? Mother was just taking the birthday cake out of the oven. It was a chocolate cake, and there would be chocolate frosting, too. "Oh, Mother," said Buddy. "May I scrape the frosting bowl?"

By three o'clock Buddy was ready. The birthday cake with its six candles was on the table. Buddy had all he could do to keep from helping himself to a little taste of the frosting.

Every few minutes he ran to the window. "When WILL they come, Mother?" he cried.

Finally, the doorbell rang.

Buddy hurried to the door. Larry and his sister Jane were there. They had a big package. Buddy opened it and found a sand toy and a musical top.

"Oh, thank you!" he cried. "Let's spin the top here in front of the fireplace."

But Buddy was kept busy answering the doorbell. The Barker twins came next. They

**Jane brought Buddy
a big package**

brought Buddy a brand-new baseball and bat.

"Oh, this is just what I've been saving pennies to buy," he said, as he thanked them.

Betty brought an indoor target game. It was fun seeing who could hit the bull's eye the most times. Mother found an extra prize—a policeman's whistle—to give to the winner. Larry won the Treasure Hunt, but no one found the peanuts in Daddy's rubbers.

Later, while they were playing "Spin the Plate," Buddy suddenly remembered something. Where was Billy Forget-Me-Not? "He told me he would come," said Buddy loud enough for his friends to hear.

"Who?" asked Larry.

"Why, Billy Forget-Me-Not."

"Who's Billy Forget-Me-Not?" asked Jackie.

Then Buddy told his friends about the little dwarf who had sat on his bedpost and talked with him. "I know he is here. He told me he would be. Let's all look for him."

"But what does he look like?" asked Larry.

"Well," answered Buddy, "his head is all white and shiny. He wears a beautiful crown, just like a king. And you should hear him sing!"

"Sing? What did he sing?" asked Joan.

"I think I can sing it for you," said Buddy.

For - get me not and you shall see

How bright and clean my face will be.

"How was he dressed?" asked Betty.

Buddy scratched his head. Then he said, "I don't remember everything he wore, but I know he had a pink collar."

"Come on," cried Jackie. "Let's all look. I want to find him."

"So do I," cried all the other children, as they started searching for Billy. They looked upstairs and downstairs. They looked in the closets, under the big tables, behind the books. Every few minutes they ran to the door, hoping to see him coming up the walk.

But they couldn't find Billy Forget-Me-Not.

"Perhaps you will find him afterwhile," said Mother. "Come; it's time to cut Buddy's cake."

As soon as the children had found their places, Buddy stood up beside the cake, closed his eyes, and whispered to himself,

"I wish, I wish, I wish I may—
Get the wish I wish today.
I wish Billy Forget-Me-Not were here."

Buddy opened his eyes, took a great big breath, and blew with all his might. PUFF! And out went the candles, every one.

"Now my wish will soon come true," said Buddy. Mother handed him the knife, and while

They ran to the door
hoping to see Billy

he cut the first piece of cake the children all sang "Happy Birthday."

When Buddy was about to take his first taste of ice cream and cake, he suddenly remembered his sore gum.

"Why, it doesn't hurt any more," he said, putting a finger into his mouth. He felt something hard. What was it?

"Look!" he cried. "I have a new tooth!"

The other boys and girls crowded around to see, and Mother said, "So that's why your gum was hurting you last night. It must be a sixth-year molar."

"I have one, too," said Henry. "My mother says it isn't a baby tooth like my others. It's a grown-up tooth." Henry tried to look important.

"Oh, I've had mine a long time," said Betty, and she tried to look grown-up. "My mother says I'll get three more sixth-year molars. Then I'll have two upstairs in my upper jaw and two downstairs in my lower jaw."

**"Look!" cried Buddy,
"I have a new tooth!"**

"Our doctor says if I drink lots of milk my teeth will be hard and strong," spoke up Jackie, and he tried to look wise. "He says we have to feed our teeth if we want them to work for us and grind up our food."

"Oho," said Buddy, and he tried to look important and grown-up and wise all at the same time. "I'll feed mine. I like milk."

"And keep them clean, too," said Mother. "A tooth is too small to wash its own face."

Buddy laughed. "Do you mean with a wash cloth, Mother?"

"Why, no, you funny boy. I mean with your toothbrush."

"But I can never remember to use my toothbrush," said Buddy.

"Well, you must learn to remember, Buddy. If you take good care of your new tooth, it will stay with you as long as you live."

After the party was over and his friends had gone home, Buddy sat down beside his sand toy.

As he turned the crank, little buckets on a chain
picked up the sand and dumped it into a red box.
Soon Buddy's head began to nod.

But just then he heard Mother say, "Come,
come, Buddy. Don't go to sleep on the floor.
Let's hop into bed. Here, I'll help you tonight."

Buddy was too tired to remember to brush
his new tooth. Even Mother forgot to remind him.

Buddy was no sooner tucked into bed than
who should appear but Billy Forget-Me-Not! He
was smoothing his pink collar just as he had done
before, but looking not quite so merry.

"Hello," he said, nodding his head so hard that
his pearl crown slipped down over his left eye.

"Oh, Billy Forget-Me-Not!" cried Buddy.
"Why didn't you come to my party? I tried and
tried to find you."

"I was there all the time," said the little dwarf,
putting his crown back in place.

"Where?" asked Buddy. "I didn't see you."

"You didn't see me, but I was there," answered

Billy. "I heard everything you said about me."

"But who are you, Billy?" cried Buddy.

"Oh, I can't tell you who I am," answered Billy. "You know what happens to dwarfs when they tell who they are. Why, they just go POOF —and disappear. No one ever sees them again. But it's all right if you GUESS who I am."

"How CAN I guess?" asked Buddy. "Can't you give me even a little hint?"

"Why, surely," said Billy. "Listen—

I work and work and work each day
So you can dance and sing and play."

He pointed his finger at Buddy. "I told you I'd be your friend and stay with you always. But you must treat me right and wash my face."

"Oh, I'll treat you right," cried Buddy. "But please tell me how I can wash your face."

But the little dwarf did not answer. He just seemed to grow smaller—and smaller—and smaller—and smaller—until he wasn't there at all.

"But you must treat me right"

Billy Gets His Face Washed

CHAPTER
THREE

EXT DAY WHEN THE mail came, there was a letter for Buddy—the first letter he had ever received. "Oh, look!" he cried proudly. "It's for me. See! This spells my name— Buddy Sharp."

"Well, well!" said Mother, almost as excited as Buddy. "It's from Grandmother Sharp down on the farm. I wonder what she can be writing to you about."

Buddy tore the envelope open and quickly
pulled out the letter. "What does it say, Mother?
What does it say?"

Buddy held his breath as Mother began to
read.

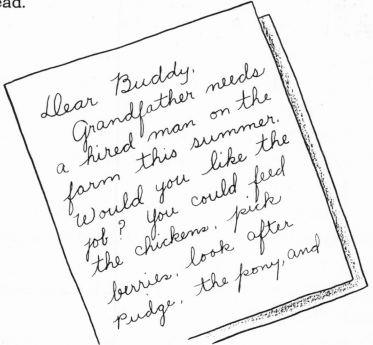

Dear Buddy,
Grandfather needs
a hired man on the
farm this summer.
Would you like the
job? You could feed
the chickens, pick
berries, look after
pudge, the pony, and

"Oh, Mother," cried Buddy, before she had fin-
ished reading, "Won't that be fun? May I go?"

"I think so, Buddy. We'll see what Daddy says."

And that's how Buddy came to spend his vacation on Grandfather's farm. Some days after breakfast he would go out to the meadow or corn-field and help Grandfather mow hay or plow corn. Or he would help Grandmother pick cherries or blackberries. Every day he went for a long ride on Pudge, the little black-and-white pony. How proud he was that he could ride without falling off!

One evening, after the day's work was done, Buddy coaxed Grandfather to let him ride one of the big work-horses.

"All right," said Grandfather. "Wait until I take Old Ned's harness off and you can ride him down to the water trough."

Buddy found Old Ned's broad back harder to stick to than little Pudge's. Twice he almost slipped off. Then he reached up and caught hold of Old Ned's mane. By the time they reached the water trough, Buddy was out on Old Ned's neck holding on for dear life. Suddenly, Old Ned low-

It was fun to
feed the chickens

ered his head into the trough. Down went Buddy —KERSPLASH! He had slid right over Old Ned's head into the water. Before Grandfather could rescue him, Buddy was soaked from head to foot. There was no more horseback-riding for Buddy that night.

Bedtime always found Buddy tired and sleepy. Many nights he had all he could do to stay awake long enough to change into his pajamas and say his prayers. And sometimes when Grandmother was busy, he would go off to bed without getting himself half clean.

One night after Buddy had gone to bed, Grandmother came to tuck him in. "Why, how dirty you are, Buddy! I don't believe you have washed yourself since breakfast. What would Mother think?"

Buddy was so ashamed of himself that he climbed out of bed without saying a word and marched off to the bathroom. For nearly a week he didn't go to bed once without giving himself

Down went Buddy —KERSPLASH!

a good washing and without brushing his teeth.

Then one night his old friend Billy Forget-Me-Not came bouncing into his room, laughing and singing for all he was worth. "Heigh-ho!" he shouted. "Look at me, Buddy. Did you ever see anyone so bright and shiny?" And before Buddy's very eyes, Billy turned handsprings all around the bed and finally hopped onto the arm of the rocking chair.

Buddy was so surprised, he hardly knew what to say. Sitting up in bed, he clapped his hands and joined in Billy's song.

Forget me not and you shall see
How bright and clean my face will be.

"Keep it up, Buddy!" the little dwarf cried. And springing into the air, he passed out of sight right through the ceiling.

The summer passed quickly for Buddy, and almost before he knew it he was back home, going to school. Now he was busier than ever, so

Buddy was glad
to go back to school

busy that he forgot all about Billy Forget-Me-Not. Then one night he saw the little dwarf perched on the head of the bed. He was so close Buddy could have reached out and touched him.

Buddy stared at him in surprise. Billy did not look fresh and clean and shining this time. His little pink collar was dirty, and his pearl crown had spots on it.

"What have you been forgetting, Buddy?" he asked, shaking his head sadly. "Why don't you wash my face?"

"How can I, when I can never find you?" asked Buddy. "If you will let me, I'll wash your face right now."

Billy shook his head so hard that his pearl crown rattled. "How can you wash my face in bed?" he asked. "I'm afraid I shall have to go away and never come back."

"Oh, please don't do that, Billy Forget-Me-Not! Please don't!"

"I can't help it," said the little dwarf. "I want

"Why don't you wash my face?"

to stay with you. All I ask is that you keep my face clean."

Suddenly, Buddy had an idea. He would capture Billy and wash his face before he could get away. Quick as a flash, he reached up and caught the little dwarf.

"Now I have you, Billy, and I'm going to wash your face."

Billy was so surprised, all he could do was shout at the top of his little voice, "Let me go! Let me go!"

But Buddy jumped out of bed and marched as fast as he could to the bathroom. He turned on the faucet and picked up the wash cloth and soap. "No! No!" cried Billy. "Not soap. You'll be sorry for this."

Buddy pretended not to hear. Mother never listened when HE didn't want to use soap.

"Oh!" cried Billy. "My poor collar! Watch out for my crown! Oh, what a terrible taste! Who ever heard of washing MY face with soap!"

**"Let me go! Let me go!"
cried Billy**

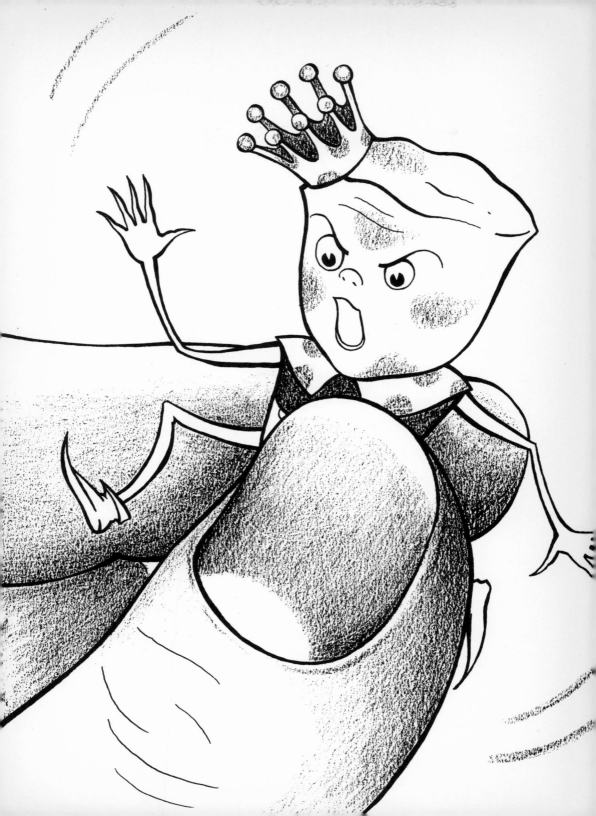

But the more Billy shouted and kicked, the harder Buddy scrubbed at his face and collar. "Now you can't say that I don't try to keep you clean," laughed Buddy.

Billy was soap-suds from head to foot, and so slippery that Buddy had all he could do to keep the little fellow from getting away. "Here, behave yourself," Buddy called. "Why are you making such a fuss? You asked me to wash your face, didn't you? Then why don't you hold still and let me do it?"

All Billy could answer was, "Ug-g . . . Bl-f-f . . . Aw-w-w . . . Glub . . . Glub."

Just as Buddy was reaching for the towel, he felt someone shaking him. Mother's voice said, "Buddy! Buddy! What are you doing up at this time of night? Why, goodness gracious! You have SOAP in your mouth!"

For a moment Buddy couldn't answer; he was still only half awake. Then he sputtered, "I . . . I . . . I . . . know it. It tastes awful."

"Here," said Mother, "rinse out your mouth.
... Now, isn't that better?"

Buddy nodded.

"What in the world were you trying to do, Buddy?"

"I was trying to wash Billy's face. He came and scolded me for not keeping him clean."

"But how did you get the soap in your mouth?"

"I don't know, Mother. I thought I was washing Billy's face," answered Buddy.

Buddy Learns Billy's Secret

CHAPTER
FOUR

UDDY WOKE UP ONE
morning to find snow on the ground. All winter
long he and his friends were busy sliding on the
ice, playing with their sleds, and building snow-
men. Then almost before he knew it, spring was
back, and Buddy and his friends were flying
their kites.

But what had become of Billy Forget-Me-
Not? In all these months Buddy had never once

**The kite string broke
and down went Buddy**

seen the little dwarf. Many a night he had listened for Billy's song. But Billy had never returned.

"If I only hadn't tried to wash his face," thought Buddy. "He told me I would be sorry. I wonder if I shall ever see him again."

At last it was almost time for Buddy's seventh birthday. He could hardly wait, for Mother had promised him another party. Larry and all his other friends were coming.

"If Billy Forget-Me-Not comes, it will be the nicest party I have ever had," thought Buddy.

But the night before the party, Buddy went to bed with a toothache.

Mother put a hot-water bag under his cheek. "If you don't get some sleep, Buddy, I'm afraid you won't be able to have your party," she said.

"Not have my party?" cried Buddy. "That's worse than a toothache!"

Poor Buddy! He thought of everything he would miss—the birthday cake with its seven candles, the ice cream, the funny paper hats, and

all the presents. His friends could not come—nor
Billy Forget-Me-Not. Buddy had to blink hard
to keep back the tears.

"Oh, why do I have to have a toothache on my
birthday?"

At last he forgot his sore tooth, and then
whom should he see but Billy Forget-Me-Not!

"Oh, Billy, I thought you would never come
back. Where have you been?"

But Billy didn't answer. He just sat on the
bedpost, holding his head. Tears ran down his
cheeks. Buddy had never seen anyone so sad.
There were brown stains on his pink collar, dirty
spots on his face, and a nick in his crown. Poor
little fellow! He didn't look as if HE could come
to the party either.

"Oh, Billy! Why do you look so sad?"

Slowly Billy raised his head. "Do you remember how bright and shiny I looked the first time
you saw me? That was just a year ago—the night
before your sixth birthday. Now look at me."

Buddy hung his head.

"This may be the last time you will ever see me," Billy continued. "I'm afraid something is going to happen. Goodbye, Buddy."

With that, he disappeared.

"Oh, Billy, Billy, don't leave me. I'll do everything you ask."

Billy didn't answer. He had gone without even singing his little song. Buddy hid his face in the pillow. He had never felt so bad in his life.

When Mother tiptoed into his room the next morning, Buddy was already up.

"Oh, are you awake so early? How is your sore tooth?" asked Mother.

Buddy tried to smile, but Mother could see that he had been crying. "I'll tell you what we'll do, Buddy. Right after breakfast let's go see the dentist. He will know how to stop the pain so you can have your party after all."

Buddy and Mother were the first ones in the dentist's office. Dr. White was a big, smiling man

"This may be the last time you will see me."

whose blue eyes seemed to twinkle all the time.

"Hello, Buddy," he called. "I haven't seen you for a long while. What's your trouble?"

"I have a sore tooth," Buddy answered.

"Let me see it," said the dentist.

He took one look at Buddy's tooth. Then he stopped smiling.

"Why, Buddy, that's your sixth-year molar. Don't you ever brush your teeth?"

"I forget to," said Buddy, hanging his head.

"But you must not forget," said the dentist, shaking his finger at Buddy just the way Billy Forget-Me-Not had done so many times. "Your teeth chew all your food. Think how hard they work for you."

Buddy lay back in the big chair and tried to listen to the dentist's voice as he worked on the tooth. But it was a warm day. Buddy had been awake so much the night before that now he began to feel very sleepy.

"I'm surprised at you, Buddy," said the dentist.

"I forget to," said Buddy,
hanging his head

"A fine tooth like that. You might have lost him.
And all he asks is that you . . ."

Buddy heard no more of what the dentist
said. He was too tired. But as he closed his eyes,
he heard another voice scolding in his ear—

"*. . . keep my face clean.*"

It was the voice of Billy Forget-Me-Not!

Buddy turned his head just in time to see the
dwarf scramble up over the edge of the dentist's
little round table. "That's just what I've been
telling you for a whole year. All I ask is that you
keep my face clean." Billy had never looked so
cross before.

As he went on scolding, Buddy suddenly
made a great discovery. Billy and the dentist were
saying the same thing! Could Billy be the tooth
Dr. White was talking about? Buddy looked at
Billy again. And then he saw it was true.

Billy was his sixth-year molar!

Buddy jumped out of the big chair and

**Billy had never
looked so cross**

danced up and down in the middle of the floor. "Oh, Billy Forget-Me-Not! Now I know who you are! Now I know who you are!"

Then he heard Mother calling, "Buddy, Buddy, what is the matter?"

Suddenly, he was wide awake. "I've found my little dwarf," he shouted, clapping his hands. "He is my sixth-year molar. All this time Billy Forget-Me-Not has been living right here in my own mouth."

Buddy could see it all now. The wish he had made on his sixth birthday had come true after all. Billy had been at the party all the time. He had worked for Buddy day by day chewing his food. He had come to Buddy in the night to scold him for forgetting to brush his teeth.

"Why didn't I guess Billy's secret before?"

"I think Billy Forget-Me-Not is going to be all right now," said Dr. White. "Just be sure you don't forget to wash his face."

"Thank you, Doctor," said Buddy. "I'll remem-

**"Forget me not and
you shall see. . . ."**

ber. Come on, Mother. Let's hurry home and get ready for the party."

So Buddy had his seventh-birthday party after all. And it was the best party he had ever had. His friends listened while he told of all his adventures with Billy Forget-Me-Not. How they laughed when Buddy told them about the time he tried to wash Billy's face!

As soon as the party was over, Buddy rushed upstairs—two steps at a time.

"Why, Buddy! Where are you going in such a hurry?" called Mother.

"To wash Billy Forget-Me-Not's face," he shouted back. And as he brushed and brushed, he thought he could hear a certain little voice gaily singing—

> *Forget me not and you shall see*
> *How bright and clean my face will be.*
> *For I'm a tooth, as now you know;*
> *So keep me brushed as white as snow.*

Billy's Song

For - get me not and you shall see

How bright and clean my face will be.

For I'm a tooth, as now you know;

So keep me brushed as white as snow.